french fries in the Park

Written by

JM Sheridan

illustrated by

Jamie forgetta

Paint the world with your own unique paintbrush!

AuthorHouse™
1663 Liberty Drive
Bloomington, IN 47403
www.authorhouse.com
Phone: 1 (800) 839-8640

Published by AuthorHouse 09/19/2017

ISBN: 978-1-5462-0963-8 (sc)
ISBN: 978-1-5462-0964-5 (e)

Library of Congress Control Number: 2017914534

Print information available on the last page.

This book is printed on acid-free paper.

authorHOUSE®

Dedication

To Brianna, Tommy and all beautiful children with autism / ASD.
May you always paint the world with your own unique paintbrush.

To Lorie, Tim, Kevin, me and all the parents of
children with autism, for being the rock our children need.

To The Autism Project, thank you for all the wonderful programs
you have for our children and families.

To Martha for your keen proofreading skills!

To Janey for her beautiful poetry. Stay creative.

To Jamie, for all of your hard work and dedication on the illustrations.

And finally, to all of my friends and family who spread the word and help
support me, a very heartfelt...
Thank you.

Be My Friend

I walk a very different path
Sometimes it's hard for me to laugh

I would also like a hug
But sometimes all I do is shrug

I want to say hi but can't begin
My clothes feel scratchy on my skin

The world is a puzzle and I don't fit
I need some space to make sense of it

I have talents that are a surprise
But when I'm frustrated I start to cry

I can play with you and do it well
But you can't rush me and please don't yell

I'm very sweet but I have a disorder
Sometimes I repeat things like a tape recorder

I arrange things neatly so I don't overload
Too much noise makes my feelings explode

I like to have fun we are truly the same
It's just that I have a different brain

If you make room for me inside of your heart
With a little patience a friendship can start

By
Janey Coyne-Scaturro
Published on Amazon and Facebook

"Are we there yet?" Brianna asked as she squirmed in her seat.

"Almost," said her dad as he smiled cheerfully.

Brianna and Mrs. Moomoo are going to the park today.
She loved the park and all the rides.
She loved the swings even more than the slides.

"We are here! We are here!" Brianna shouted with glee.

She could see the big, red swing set down by the tall oak trees.

The moment Brianna's dad unbuckled her seat,
she grabbed Mrs. Moomoo and ran fast on her feet.
"Slow down!" he called to her, as he juggled their things.

But Brianna did not slow down.
She could not slow down.
She held tight to Mrs. Moomoo as her feet thumped on the ground.

When Brianna arrived at the swings,
she pulled to a stop.
There was a boy standing there
with shiny black hair.
He was looking at the ground
and waving his hands in the air.

"Don't be afraid," said the boy's dad.
"He's just excited. He's not mad."
"Tommy loves the swings most of all," he said,
"but we need to make sure he's buckled in so he doesn't fall."

"Why is he waving his hands?" Brianna asked.
"Tommy has autism," the man replied. "Hand waving is called stimming.
It helps him control his emotions inside."

"Swing please," Tommy said to his dad.
"Okay Tommy," said the man.
"Hold on tight, and I'll swing you as high as I can."

"Here we go!"
Brianna cheered out loud, as she and Mrs. Moomoo
soared into the clouds.

All too soon the swing began to slow down.
"Time for a snack," said Brianna's dad
as he placed her on the ground.

"Hi," Brianna said
as she sat down at the table.
But the boy did not look up.
He did not say hello.
"Is that your dog?"
she asked nice and slow.

"This is Shadow," Tommy's dad introduced the dog.
"He's Tommy's very best friend,
and he even plays leapfrog!"

"Children with autism can't look you in the eye,"
explained Tommy's dad.
"It's not that he doesn't like you,
so please don't be sad."

"Fries!" Tommy said with a hearty burst.
"I have fries, too!" Brianna said with a smile,
then she gave Mrs. Moomoo one from her pile.

After Brianna and Tommy finished their fries,
they headed back to the playground
to ride the wobbly butterflies.

They played side by side all through the day.
And even though the boy did not speak,
Brianna knew he was having fun by his laughter and rosy cheeks.

"Time to head home," said Brianna's dad.
"Say good-bye to Tommy while I pack our bags."

Thump! Whump! Brianna almost fell down.
"Easy, Tommy," said his dad.
"Not everyone likes a strong squeeze like you."
"Please say good-bye to Brianna and Mrs. Moomoo."

"I had fun playing with Tommy today," Brianna said.
"And Daddy, did you see?" she asked.
"Tommy loves French fries just like me.'

The End

CPSIA information can be obtained
at www.ICGtesting.com
Printed in the USA
BVOW05s0017270917
496008BV00006B/12/P

9 781546 209638